W9-BAQ-651

The Ugly Duckling

A Folk & Fairy Tale Reader

retold by Liza Charlesworth
illustrated by Ian Smith

ISBN 978-0-545-76732-3

12 11   17 18 19

Printed in the U.S.A.   40
First printing, September 2014

Designed by Maria Mercado

SCHOLASTIC INC.

Once upon a time,
four ducklings were born.
Crack, crack, crack, crack!

Three of the ducklings were
yellow and cute.
One was gray and ugly.

"Go away," said the cute ducklings.
"You are ugly."

So the ugly duckling went away.
Swim, swim, swim.
He was very sad.

By and by, he met some pink birds.
"Can I stay with you?" he asked.
"No. You are too ugly," they said.

So the ugly duckling went away.
Swim, swim, swim.
He was very sad.

By and by, he met some blue birds.
"Can I stay with you?" he asked.
"No. You are too ugly," they said.

So the ugly duckling went away.
Swim, swim, swim.
He was very sad.

The ugly duckling cried and cried.
He also grew and changed.

One day, he met some tall, white birds.
Oh my, they were so pretty!

"Why are you sad?" they asked.
"Because I am ugly," he said.
"Look in the water," they said.

So the ugly duckling did.
Oh my, he had changed a lot!
He was a pretty swan just like them.

"Do you want to live with us?"
they asked.
"Oh yes!" said the ugly duckling.

Then he went away with the swans.
Swim, swim, swim.
And they all swam happily ever after.

Comprehension Boosters

1. How did the yellow, pink, and blue birds treat the ugly duckling?

2. How did the ugly duckling feel at the beginning of the story? How did he feel at the end? Why?

3. The swans were kind. Use three more words to describe them.